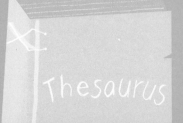

Flibbertigibbet!

Irate

Shenanigans!

Onomatopoeia!

Thesaurus
Thesaurus
Cantankerous
Forlorn
Thesaurus
Thesaurus
Exhausted
Thesaurus
Confused
Thesaurus

Theo TheSaurus

The Dinosaur Who Loved Big Words

Written by
Shelli R. Johannes

Illustrated by
Mike Moran

PHILOMEL BOOKS

Today was **migration** day.

Migration means to move from one place to another.

DEFINO-DINO

Theo's parents were ecstatic.

Theo was not.

That's because Theo was a TheSaurus.

He loved big words.

The more **colossal**, the better!

But at a new school, his big words might get in the way.

"How will I make friends if no one understands me?"
he asked his parents.

"Communicating with new acquaintances can be challenging for a TheSaurus," said his mom.

"We know you will work hard to make new companions," said his dad.

Theo wasn't convinced.

At school, his teacher introduced him. "Class, this is Theo."

The class chanted, "Hello, Theo."

"Salutations!" he shouted back.

No one had ever met a TheSaurus before.

So they had a **plethora** of questions.

Some hurt more than others.

Theo explained his species the best he could.

"TheSauruses are the only **logomaniacs** on the planet."

Logomaniacs means they are "word lovers" or "word obsessed."

DEFINO-DINO

But his classmates looked confused.

Theo got an idea!

He would teach everyone all about TheSauruses.

Then maybe they'd understand him and want to be his friend.

Theo began by sharing some of his TheSaurus vocabulary.

Onomatopoeia!

Shenanigans!

Flibbertigibbet!

But his classmates weren't impressed.

Misunderstandings could be frustrating.

And lonely.

Theo had another idea. He would read them his favorite book!

"Could someone walk me to the **athenaeum**?" he asked.

Athenaeum is another word for library.

DEFINO-DINO

His classmates walked him to the auditorium instead.

Misinterpretations could be confusing.

And risky.

During lunch, Theo offered some of his homemade snacks.

"Would anyone like to try my special crudités?"

Misconceptions could be tough to swallow.

And bitter.

At recess, Theo tried something else.

He suggested they all play a simple game together.

"Would anyone like to engage in a round of **conceal-and-search**?"

Conceal-and-search is another way of saying hide-and-seek.

DEFINO-DINO

His classmates started a game of tag instead.

Miscommunications could be dangerous.

And painful.

But Theo was determined to find a way.

On Friday, he communicated in writing instead.

I request your attendance to celebrate the anniversary of my hatching.

Finally, the time came!

Theo waited.

And waited.

And waited.

He tried to look on the bright side.

"**Supplementary** snacks for me!"

But it wasn't that simple.

Playing alone wasn't any fun.

"Can you explain how you're feeling?" his mom asked.

Theo tried to find the best word to describe his emotions.

Exhausted
Forlorn
Confused
Cantankerous
Irate

But he didn't know what to say.

Because no word seemed to fit.

For the first time ever, Theo was speechless.

Luckily, his parents knew just what to do.

Because sometimes, Theo didn't need any words at all.

Then the doorbell rang.

"**Salutations**!" his new friends shouted.

And that was *exactly* the word Theo needed to hear.

In Theo's Words . . .

Acquaintances—people you meet

Athenaeum—library

Attendance—presence at an event

Cantankerous—bad tempered, grumpy, or looking for an argument

Colossal—extra big

Companions—friends

Confused—can't think clearly or have difficulty in understanding

Crudités—raw food

Ecstatic—extra happy

Exhausted—extra tired

Flibbertigibbet—a flighty or whimsical person

Forlorn— sad and desperate

Irate—mad or angry

Logomaniac—someone who loves words

Migration—move

Miscommunication—failure to communicate clearly

Misconception—an incorrect view

Misinterpretation—an incorrect explanation of something

Misunderstanding—an incorrect understanding of something

Onomatopoeia—a word that describes a sound, like *hoot*

Plethora—a whole lot

Salutations—hello

Shenanigans—mischief or mischievous play

Supplementary—extra

To Mom and Dad, for teaching me the most important word of all: love —S.J.

To every single frontline hero! Thank you! —M.M.

PHILOMEL BOOKS

An imprint of Penguin Random House LLC, New York

First published in the United States of America by Philomel, an imprint of Penguin Random House LLC, 2021.

Text copyright © 2021 by Shelli Johannes.

Illustrations copyright © 2021 by Mike Moran.

Philomel Books is a registered trademark of Penguin Random House LLC.

Visit us online at penguinrandomhouse.com.

Library of Congress Cataloging-in-Publication Data is available.

Manufactured in China

ISBN 9780593205518

1 3 5 7 9 10 8 6 4 2

Edited by Liza Kaplan. • Design by Monique Sterl
Text set in Horley Old Style

Art created in Photoshop, Procreate, and mixed me

Thesaurus

Thesaurus

Cantankerous

esaurus

Forlorn

Thesaurus

Thesaurus

Exhausted

esaurus

Thesaurus

Confused

Thesaurus

Thesaurus